Aunt Chip and the Great

Triple Creek Dam Affair

PATRICIA POLACCO

A TRUMPET CLUB SPECIAL EDITION

Absolutely everybody in Triple Creek loved their TV sets. No one could remember a time when there wasn't a TV in every home. Nor could they remember when they weren't watching TV.

Their TV's were always on. While they ate their meals. While they worked. While they played. While they slept. They even kept photos of their TV's on their mantels along with all the pictures of their family members.

Everyone loved their TV's, except Eli's Aunt Charlotte. Aunt Chip, as Eli called her, didn't even own a TV! As a matter of fact, she had NEVER owned one.

This made her suspect in the eyes of the townsfolk of Triple Creek, especially since she had "upped" and taken to her bed well over fifty years ago and vowed never to get out of it again. No one knew why, really, though there was some talk that it happened just about the time that huge TV tower was built over on Cedar and Oak.

"I'm takin' to my bed, ain't never gittin' up again!" they say she shouted out of her window. "But there will be consequences...mark my words. There will be consequences." And she settled into her eiderdown.

Eli loved his Aunt Charlotte very much, in spite of her strange ways. He visited her almost every day. He especially loved when she would start into one of her great stories. Like the one about the little kid in Holland who held back the sea by putting his thumb in the dike or his favorite about a great white whale that lived in the deepest, darkest part of the ocean.

"Where do all them stories come from, Aunt Chip?" he asked one day.

"Some come out of thin air. Some come out of my dreams. Some come right out of books!"

"Books?" Eli thought for a long time. "How do you get a story from a book?"

"Whatever do you mean, HOW, child?"

"I mean we USE books all the time. They're all over town, but . . ."

"Use them? You mean, READ them, don't you?" she asked, leaning closer to the boy.

"R-r-read? What's that?" Eli asked.

"I knew it! I knew there'd be consequences!" Aunt Chip hissed as she threw off her covers and, for the first time in fifty years, let one foot touch the floor.

"Child, git me my clothes," she ordered.

"How come you're gittin' up, Aunt Chip?" Eli asked.

"'Cause I suspect there's a wrong that needs to be put right," she said, "and I've got to see what's happened for myself."

Eli and Aunt Chip walked into the center of town. Eli was right. Books were being well used. For doorstops, to hold up roofs, to sit on, to eat off, to sleep under, to mend fences, to stuff potholes, to prop up sagging buildings, and even to shore up the dam.

"Where has everyone gone?" Aunt Chip asked in stunned amazement. "There aren't any children playin'. I don't hear talkin' or laughin'."

"Everyone's watchin'," Eli answered with authority. "It's almost time for a cliff-hangin' episode of *How the Dawn Churns*."

"There *have been* consequences, indeed!" Aunt Chip said.

Then, as they reached the corner of Cedar and Oak, Aunt Chip's eyes beheld the steel-strutted TV tower. She choked with tears. "Take me home, boy. I've seen enough!"

That afternoon they sat together in front of the fire sipping very strong tea.

"Do you want to know what glory used to be on the corner of Cedar and Oak?"

"What, Aunt Chip?" Eli climbed up next to her.

"That's where the library used to be," she said.

"What's a library?" Eli asked.

"It's a place where books used to be kept, a long time ago," she answered wistfully.

"Why did they keep books in a building?" Eli asked.

"They kept them there for folks to borrow and take home to read. Look, child," and she went to a cabinet covered with cobwebs, took out a book, and opened it for him. Dust fluttered out of its pages. "Now look at this. Those are words. They tell about ideas, dreams, and feelings. They take you to places far from here. They show you how to be fair and just, and sometimes show you what happens when you're not. Books are a treasure. All you need is the key."

"The key?" Eli asked.

"The key! Knowin' these words and their meanings," she answered softly. "It's called readin'."

"But, Aunt Chip, if the library had all those treasures, why would anyone take it away?"

"Wellsir," she started, "folks got so taken up by those TV's that they came to the library less and less. Pretty soon folks started to forget what it was there for. All except the librarian. She was there, all right, every single day.

"Folks started callin' her mad for sittin' in that empty old building day after day. Finally they carried her away, crazy as a March hare, everyone said. She was tryin' to stop the wrecking ball. But it still crashed into the walls and flattened the place. Then that giant TV tower came."

Eli looked again at the open book they both held in their hands. "I want to read, Aunt Chip. Can you teach me?"

"Of course, child," she said as she hugged him up.

Now, Eli took to reading like a beaver takes to gnawing wood, or a flea takes to a dirty little yella dog. Within weeks he could read just about everything. And he did. He read labels on cereal boxes, covers on canned goods at the store, road signs, all those things folks had memorized by their shapes.

It wasn't long before his little classmates at school, where TV sets had long since replaced teachers, noticed that he knew what things said on labels, covers, and such.

"Look, Eli can hear things that we can't," Celeste Appleby said one day. Eli was reading a peanut-butter cookie recipe from one of Aunt Chip's cookbooks.

"How come we can't hear what you are a-hearin' when we look at this book?" Hollis Lonsberry asked.

"I'm not a-hearin' it," Eli said. "I'm a-readin' it. It's kind of like I can see it talkin'."

"Read more!" the other children clamored, and each one grabbed a book from a nearby pothole and held it up in front of Eli.

Eli read about a princess in a kingdom, he read about isosceles triangles, and he read about the sinking of the *Titanic*. At last one boy announced, "We want to read too, Eli." And they all cheered, "Yes!" That's when Eli took the children to Aunt Chip.

"All right, all right," she said when they asked, "but I don't have enough books! We'll need more."

That's when the children started borrowing books from all over town. They took them out of potholes. Off fences. From the tops of roofs. Out from under sagging buildings. They borrowed and borrowed. They got them from everywhere they could find them.

Pretty soon Aunt Chip's house echoed with small voices reading from *Aesop's Fables* and *Grimm's Fairy Tales*, and stories by Hans Christian Andersen and Charles Dickens. Now those children couldn't get enough!

One day Eli and his friends were passing under a very tall wall made almost entirely of books on the edge of town. The original wall had crumbled and the townsfolk had rebuilt it. Eli was reading the spines of each book in the wall, when his eye caught the gold lettering of a lovely green one.

"Help me up so I can reach it." He could hardly wait to touch it. The children stood on each other's shoulders until Eli's fingers could finally reach the book.

"*Moby Dick*," he exclaimed as he pried it loose.

Moby Dick sloshed out of the wall with a watery, wet FFFFFPPLLLLLU-UUUNNNNKKKSSSSHHH. "Got it!" he said. That was when they all heard a low, rumbling sound that grew louder and louder. They looked up and noticed a trickle of water coming out from where *Moby Dick* had been.

The trickle got bigger and bigger. The rumbling got louder and louder. The ground under their feet started to shake, and they noticed that they were ankle-deep in water.

"Let's get to the bluff!" Eli called out.

When they reached the bluff and looked down, they saw it: The wall of books had become the new Triple Creek Dam, and it was bowing under the weight of the lake behind it. Then with a thundering, watery roar, it EXPLODED.

The explosion sent the books flying straight up. They hurtled so high into the air that they disappeared clean out of sight. Tons of water surged down past Dead Man's Bluff and past the Bucket of Suds Saloon and was heading straight for the TV tower next to the bridge at Cedar and Oak streets.

The wall of water hit that tower with such force that it crumpled up like tinfoil.

When the children got into town, they saw all the grown-ups walking around, looking confused and dazed. "My TV went off . . . for no reason at all," a woman said as she grasped the photo of her TV to her chest.

"I can't live without my sports recap of the replay of Sunday's game," a hysterical man screamed as he collapsed with a serious case of the vapors.

"Who could have done such a thing to our town!" the mayor called out in anguish, clutching his remote control.

"It's all my fault," Eli finally said above the din. Aunt Chip came and stood by his side. "All I wanted to do was read this book." Eli held up the copy of *Moby Dick*.

"Read? Did you say READ?" the mayor said as the townsfolk recoiled in disbelief.

"Why, folks haven't done that around here since, why, since I can remember."

"If we were meant to read, we woulda been born bein' able to do it!"

"It must be bad if'n doin' it made the dam break and take out the TV tower!" The crowd roared in agreement.

"Just who taught you to read?" the mayor asked as he drew closer to Eli. Eli gestured to Aunt Chip. There was a collective gasp.

"I knew it.... I've heard stories about her!" a voice said. "Crazy old coot!" a man hissed.

"She isn't crazy!" Eli screamed.

All of the children came out from the crowd and surrounded Aunt Chip.

"She's been teaching all of us to read!"

"So we've been borrowing books from all over town," Eli said.

"That's where they've been disappearing to," a mean-looking woman snapped. "You'll just have to put them all back."

"They'll do nothing of the kind!" Aunt Chip said with resolve. "Fifty years ago, I didn't have the strength to stand up to the city fathers. But now I do!" she said as she locked hands with the children.

Eli looked up at his Aunt Chip. "It was you.... You were the librarian. That's why you took to bed."

"If'n we were meant to read, there surely would have been a sign," the town soothsayer said as she gazed at the horizon.

Wellsir, exactly at that very moment all them books that had been blown out of the dam started to fall right out of the sky.

"Look!" a child said excitedly. "It's raining books!"

Sure enough, as the crowd looked skyward, down came a shower of books. Fairy tales, classics, dictionaries, encyclopedias, fiction, non-fiction…. Black books, brown ones, green ones, red ones, leather-bound, canvas-backed, paperback…. Books, books, and more books.

"This is a miracle!" the town soothsayer exclaimed.

For the first time in years, the townsfolk were filled with the wonder that only a child knows. They embraced one another and danced with joy that such a glorious thing had happened to them. Clearly it was a sign!

But the miraculous event had taken their eyes off their TV screens long enough for them finally to see what their town had become.

"I had no idea," the mayor said sadly.

"I told them there'd be consequences," Aunt Chip said. "But you can change all this. Get to reading again, Titus," she said to him. "That's a start!"

"But none of us knows how to read," a very large man said as he stepped out from the crowd.

A little girl came up to him. "I'll teach you, Daddy," she said quietly as she took his hand.

Then one by one, the townsfolk stepped forward, and one by one, they were joined by their children or grandchildren, a chorus of small voices saying the same thing over and over: "I'll teach you, Momma." "I'll teach you, Papa."

Wellsir, Triple Creek wasn't the same after that glorious day. Folks were fixin' up their homes and rebuilding, thanks to the books on remodeling and building that they were reading. They were planting gardens and parks because of books on gardening. And they were sitting on their front porches again, and talking to one another. Rousing conversations and laughter could be heard everywhere, as folks talked about magazines, books, and newspapers.

Understand, folks still had their TV's, all right, but they were wise about what they watched and for how long. They had so much else to do!

And people began moving to Triple Creek in droves. A Chinese restaurant, a theater, and a movie house that brought in movies from as far away as Moose Jaw, clear in the upper peninsula, opened! Giovanni Gorganzola, the world-renowned tenor, came and started a real opera company.

Finally a new school was built where the old one had stood, with real teachers and lots and lots of books! Including a 322-page book, *Moby Dick*.

But the folks were most proud of their new library. Do you know the ribbon-cutting ceremony attracted dignitaries from all over the country? Including Jubilation T. Fogbound, the great senior senator from our great state of Michigan. But it was the mayor who escorted the new town librarian into the new building and sat her at her desk, personally. She, once again, took her rightful place, which had been hers fifty years before.

Now I said that a great many stories are true, though some may not have happened. You'll have to judge for yourself about this one. But next time you hear about a library being closed, you'll know that there will be consequences. And if you hear folks say that there won't be, just have them read this-here book.

As for Eli. Well, he grew up, went off to college, and studied journalism. He came back to Triple Creek about eight years ago and started the town newspaper. He called it the Triple Creek Herald Consequence. I've heard that that little paper won an international award for first-class journalism and excellence just last year. He keeps the trophy right there on the shelf behind him, next to a tattered, well-loved copy of Moby Dick.

To stubborn librarians everywhere,
but most especially to two educators
and advocates for the minds of children:
my mother, Mary Ellen Gaw Barber and
my friend, Dr. Charlotte S. Huck.
And to one great kid,
Michael Christopher Molesky.

Book design by Donna Mark. Text set in Garth Graphic.

ISBN 0-590-10250-8

12 11 10 9 8 7   2/0

Printed in the U.S.A.   14

First Scholastic printing, April 1997